Say Your ABCs with Me

ILLUSTRATIONS BY GRANNY B & DALL-E AI

Learn more at Grannybbooks.com

SAY YOUR ABCS WITH ALL THE ANIMALS

Suitable for All Ages

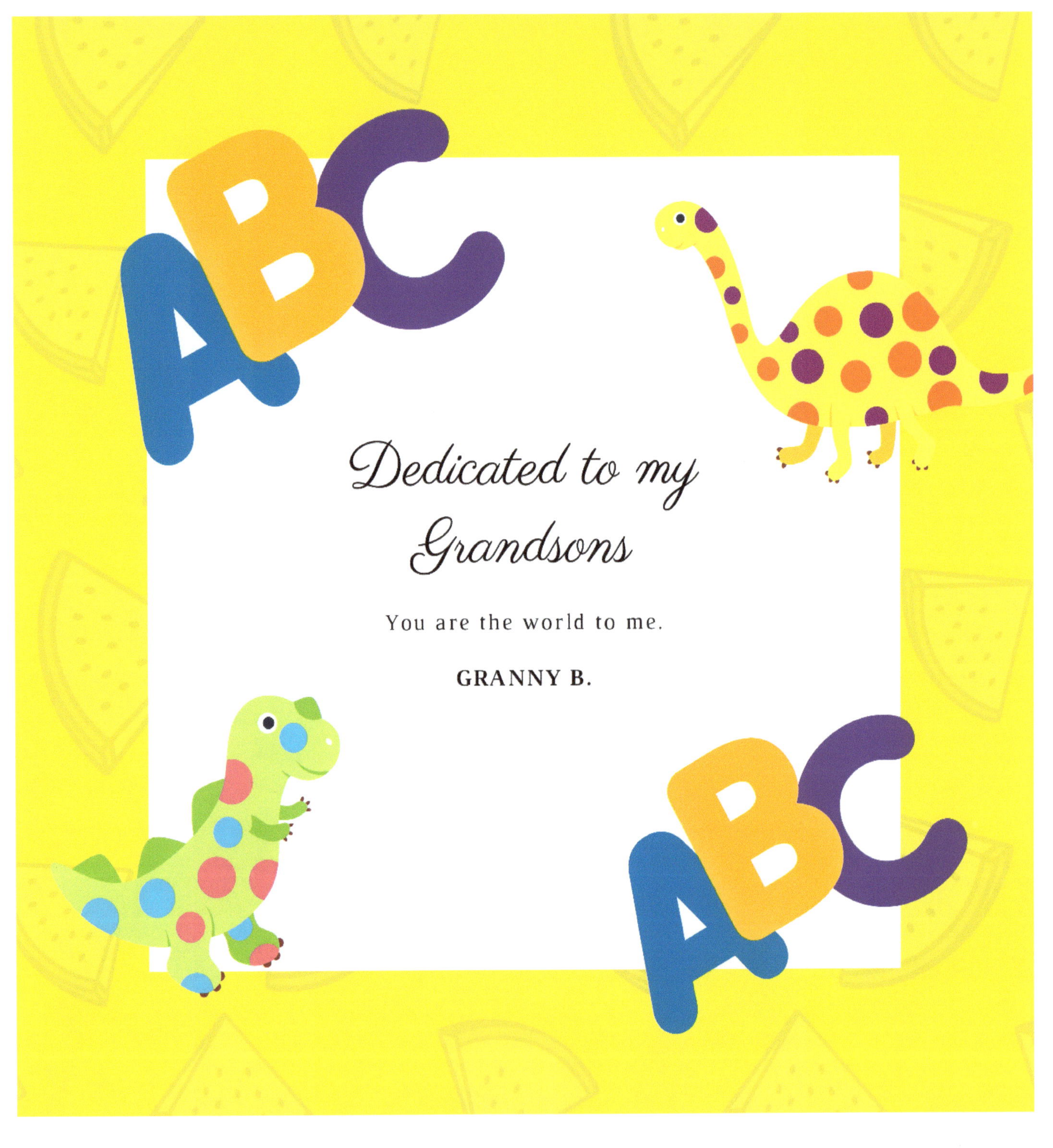

Dedicated to my Grandsons

You are the world to me.

GRANNY B.

A is for apples, and
alligators too!

B is for books, and little bears that like to read them!

C is for cookies, and carrots that taste delicious at a tea party!

D is for ducks and
dogs that like to play
with them!

E is for eggs, and elephant. Do elephants eat eggs?

F is for flowers and fish. Do
gold fish like the smell of
tulips?

G is for grapes, and giraffes that like to eat them!

H is for horses, hippos and hay which they like to eat.

I is for ice cream, and iguanas. What kind of ice cream do you like?

J is for jellybeans, and
jaguars . What's your
favorite flavor of jellybean?

K is for kites, and
kittens that like to play
with them!

L is for lemons and lions. Do lions like lemons? Do you?

M is for mice and the
monkeys that like to play
with them!

N is for nuts, and nurses who like to eat them at snack time.

O is for octopus and sweet
juicy oranges.

P is for pigs, potatoes, and pie! What is your favorite kind of pie?

Q is for quails, and queen bees.

R is for roses and rabbits
that like to smell them!

S is for sunflowers, and snakes. What is your favorite flower?

T is for turtles, and tigers
having fun in the forest

U is for umbrellas and
unicorns that like to hide
under them!

V is for violets, and vampires that like to sniff them.

W is for whales, waffles
and wolves!

X is for xylophones, and
xenomorphs that like to
play them.

Y is for yogurt, yo-yo
and Yak.

Z is for zebras and zucchini muffins. Do zebras eat zucchini?

Say Your ABCs with Me!

A B C D E F G H I J K L M
N O P Q R S T U V W X Y Z

by Granny B with Jasper AI

Illustrations by Granny B. & DALL-E

Human & AI Creating Magic Together

The End
Granny B.

www.ingramcontent.com/pod-product-compliance
Lightning Source LLC
LaVergne TN
LVHW071130160826
845679LV00005B/1236
9798846159020